D1063817

Copyright © 1987 Victoria House Publishing Ltd.
This edition published by Gallery Books,
an imprint of W. H. Smith Publishers Inc.,
112 Madison Avenue, New York,
New York 10016.

Produced for Gallery Books by Victoria House
Publishing Ltd., Bath, England.

ISBN 0-8317-4485-5

Printed in Portugal.

MIP and MOP

Written by Gerald Hawksley
Illustrated by Colin King

GALLERY BOOKS
An Imprint of W. H. Smith Publishers Inc.
112 Madison Avenue
New York City 10016

This is Mip.

This is Mip's and Mop's favorite ball. Sneaky Rat is hiding it.

This is Mop.

Mip and Mop want
to play with their
favorite ball,
but they can't
find it
anywhere.

''I'll help look for your ball, Mip and Mop,'' says the hedgehog.

Mop is looking in the flower bed. He can't find the ball.

Mip is looking
in the bushes.
He can't find
the ball.

"I'd help you look for your ball,
Mip and Mop," says the owl,
"but I've lost my
spectacles."

"I'll try looking
upside down,"
says the owl.

Mop looks for the ball
behind a tree.

Mip looks for the ball in the garden shed.

The hedgehog looks for the ball in the vegetable patch.

"I've found some flowerpots," says the hedgehog.

"Look what I've found," says Mop.

"Look what I've found!" says Mip.

The owl flies down
from the tree.

"My spectacles!"
cries the owl.
"Thank you, Mop."

"Goodness! My old hat!" cries the hedgehog. "Thank you, Mip."

The owl can see the whole garden from the top of the tree. ''Sneaky Rat has got the ball,'' he calls.

''I can see Sneaky Rat,'' says Mop.

"Sneaky Rat
looks sad,"
says Mip.

Sneaky Rat is peeking out
from behind a bush.

"It was Sneaky Rat who hid my spectacles," says the owl.

"Sneaky Rat, Sneaky Rat, hid my hat!" calls the hedgehog.

"Sneaky Rat wants to be friends,"
say Mip and Mop.

"Nobody would
play with me,"
says Sneaky Rat,
"so I hid everything."

"I'm sorry I hid
your things,"
says Sneaky Rat.

"You should have asked, Sneaky Rat," says
the hedgehog. "We'd have played with you."

"Sneaky Rat didn't mean any harm," says the owl.

"Let's play catch," says Mip.

Mop throws the ball high in the air.